PRAISE FOR EVERY DARK CLOUD

"Part enchanting dreamworld, part blistering nightmare, Every Dark Cloud warns us of humanity's worst impulses, and reminds us of its best."

— STEPHANIE FELDMAN, AUTHOR OF
SATURNALIA

"Marisca Pichette's *Every Dark Cloud* is a spare, unflinching, yet wonderfully compassionate window into a future that feels all too possible - but even in the darkness of late-stage capitalism taken to its (un)natural extreme, Pichette never loses sight of human connection, both to each other and to the natural world. It's a quick, fully realized read with its fingers planted firmly in the soil, delightfully queer sensibilities, and characters I would gladly follow far beyond these pages."

— JAQ EVANS, AUTHOR OF *WHAT GROWS
IN THE DARK*

"Part dystopia, part horror, Pichette has created an inventive and emotionally evocative world where profound and unsettling truths are held in light and darkness. *Every Dark Cloud* is a gripping, genre-defying novella shot-through with beauty and sporror."

"Lyrical, graceful, and dark -- Marisca Pichette's *Every Dark Cloud* is a marvel of climate fiction. Pichette pulls off an absolute coup by creating an immersive world that delights even as it terrifies, down to the sentence-level. But don't be fooled. This eerie world is not some far-off, hypothetical dream land of elsewhere. Pichette's novella dares us to stare directly at our future, in the tradition of the very best speculative fiction: by interrogating a possible future, we can most clearly see our present."

EVERY DARK CLOUD

EVERY DARK CLOUD

MARISCA PICHETTE

GHOST ORCHID PRESS

Every Dark Cloud

First published in Great Britain 2025 by Ghost Orchid Press

ISBN (paperback): 978-1-7390918-9-7

ISBN (e-book): 978-1-7390918-8-0

Cover illustration © Carly Allen-Fletcher

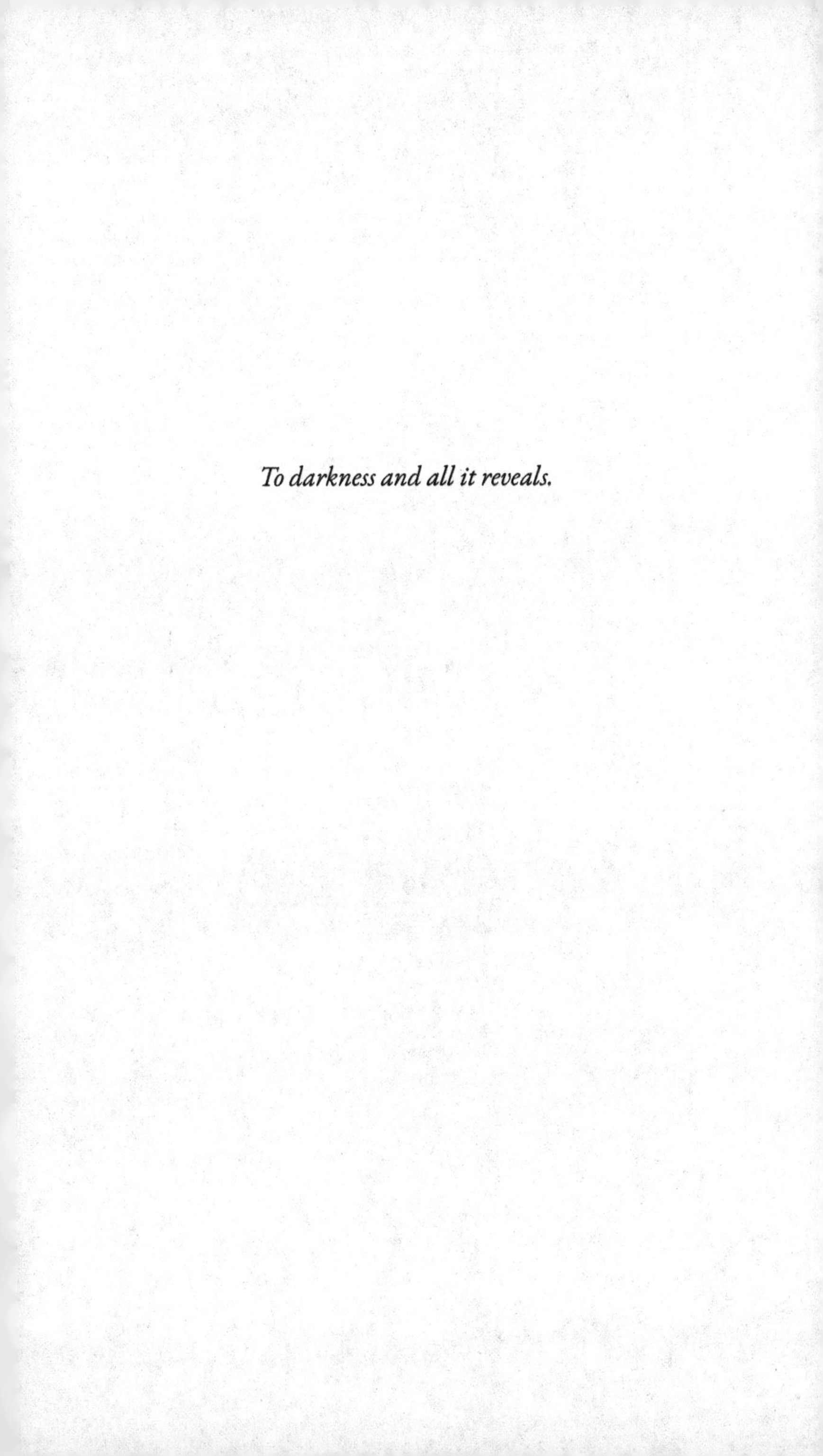

To darkness and all it reveals.

There is no color in a darkness world. Without light to illuminate, reflect, and identify, we will all be shadows and sounds.

There is no day without a sun.
There is no night without a moon.
There is only the air we breathe.

FROM *THE ACTS OF CLOUDING*, RATIFIED
BY THE UNITED GOVERNMENTS AT THE
FOUNDING OF THE COALITION

EVERY DARK CLOUD

WE ALL KNOW THE HISTORY. How grass used to be green, clouds were once white, nights broken by hours of day. The BioHomes database is overflowing with photos, videos, and 3D reproductions of cities and nations that no longer exist in the same way. When I started my career I studied them, trying to understand exactly how they worked—but those old construction modes don't matter now. None of my designs look anything like the past.

I draw my fingers across the table screen, vibrations responding to my touch. In near total darkness, I construct a building in virtual dimensions.

My right hand draws on the pad, larger and more versatile than the one I have at home. My left hand traces the contours of the clay model I sculpted while designing this latest complex.

With each new virtual layer, I stop and record calculations at the bottom of the screen. I rely primarily on the subtle vibrations to track my progress, but the screen does emit a dim light, bright enough to show me variations in shadow. I pause, cracking my right wrist. I've been working at the desk for hours. My back is starting to seize up.

BioHomes isn't the only architectural conglomerate in this region. However, it's certainly the biggest, richest, and oldest. It was founded just a year after the Clouding.

I wasn't yet born when the clouds rolled in. I only know the history, taught in school and remembered in audio files linked to the Coalition database. Disaster unfurled in the form of creeping heat and droughts without reprieve. Accounts abound of scorching light, thinning ozone, brittle crops, and peeling skin. Wildfires spread where they shouldn't, and wars divided an already pockmarked planet. It might've been the end for us. It almost was.

I glance up from my worktable, my thoughts drifting to stories of ceaseless light, charred skin; the stench of singed hair and putrefying meat. The world before the Clouding verged on apocalypse.

And so, eighty years ago, humanity was faced with a choice: allow the sun to burn everything and everyone, or cover the sky—plunging the world into darkness. After years fighting worsening radiation, cancers, and fires spreading from one population to another, the Coalition decided on darkness.

They built towers across the hemispheres, dwarfing the skyscrapers that had once stood tall and proud, now melted and uninhabitable. Artificial lights sold out in each country as populations prepared to be locked in eternal shadow. Not midnight, not the blackness that precedes dawn. The Clouding was expected to be something else. Akin to the depths of caves that have never once known daylight. The abyssal plain, which has never known stars. That's what the United Governments expected when they formed the Coalition.

While I rest my eyes, staring into the ambient dark, I run

my finger along the base of the screen, activating an audio file. Jayde's voice fills the empty workspace. I'm the only one here.

"*BioHomes Complex No. 25683-80-9063.18, residential grade. Designer assigned to project: Mallory Myco. Project due date: June 18th.*"

More than four weeks away. I increase the brightness on the screen enough to view my digital floor plan in detail. I spin it around, my left hand following the lines of the clay model, comparing them. My entire life—nearly thirty years—has been spent in darkness. I rely on touch and sound more than sight. Even the dimmest LEDs leave light echoes dancing in my eyes. I turn away, squinting at my sculpture.

I've finished the basic structure, at least. I can design the inside on my smaller pad at home.

I save my progress and switch off the screen, waiting for my eyes to readjust to perpetual gloom. When my senses are settled, I pick up the clay model and bring it to the rack, sliding it into place next to the other projects. Several are mine; the rest belong to the other designers on staff. A scattered array of labels adorn half the models; Jayde has already been by to appraise those and left their feedback. I push down a flicker of unease. Jayde usually approves of my designs. Still, with every new project, I wonder if I'm on the right track.

I don't need to see to find my way through the empty office and outside, stepping into the cloud of fragrance generated by the senselens at the door: concrete and clean plastic. I didn't choose the scent BioHomes uses to identify its workspaces. While apt, the concoction is bland in my nose. I'm glad to leave it behind me, following the smooth ramp down to the edge of the woods. No modern buildings have been designed with steps since the Clouding.

As I walk, a warm breeze tickles my cheeks. I close my eyes, breathing the darkness. The air is moist and filtered, oxygen pumped steadily from the nearest greenhouse. The same artificialights that grow the food we eat cultivate breathable air beneath the thick layer of cloud. I open my eyes and gaze up at the impenetrable darkness overhead.

The Coalition's towers still stand, the nearest a few miles from these woods. I've visited the bases on a few occasions. They hum, wires sprawling like vines planting themselves in the earth. These bring energy throughout the remade world. Solar energy, powerful and renewable—from a light so bright, it almost killed us.

Walking in darkness, I think about the brilliant artificialights installed in every complex. I've designed them plenty of times. Often, they're set to the lowest brightness. But any can be increased to painful whiteness, a beam that cuts through the comfortable dark, exposing everything in its path in sharp detail. Light echoes linger when I close my eyes.

My bare feet bring me from concrete onto cool soil. Dew slicks my skin. Artificialights may be bright, but they're never hot. They won't burn what they touch, as the sun did. Everyone's seen photos of the damage the sun caused before the Clouding.

Mushrooms bend under my toes, releasing their spores to the ever-night. The darkness around me is no longer absolute.

Following the Clouding, something emerged the Coalition did not anticipate. A piece of the world never seen before, now as ubiquitous as the clouds.

Color didn't vanish from the landscape. It grew in new ways. Beautiful ways.

Blue glitters before me, a sparkling line through the trees. Around it, pale patches of fungal green. Bioluminescence once too faint for human eyes to catch now thrives in the altered world.

I step into the soft embrace of a light that doesn't burn.

THE PATH through the dead forest vibrates at a low frequency. I can hear it—like the towers, but quieter. Calmer. The sensation of walking on it keeps me on track, my feet tingling with tiny, measured tremors. But the main reason for the vibrating design is illumination.

The air above the path shimmers in pulses of soft blue. With each vibration, bacteria luminesce, sparkling around my feet. The motion of my body is too slow, too irregular to activate them. It took years of careful design before the optimal frequency was discovered.

Light is not gone. Light lives in the very air we breathe.

I walk slowly, watching the bacteria unspooling in swirls of azure. Sometimes I'm too preoccupied to pay attention to them, hurrying home with numbers spinning in my head. I think this is how it happened, almost a century ago. Those people didn't feel there was time to look at their feet; to recognize what grew with the aid of the sun above them. I wonder sometimes if they noticed what was dying, like them, because of the weakened atmosphere. Did they notice crisped plants and boiled animals? They must have.

I wonder also if they noticed the other things—creatures that adapted better. Minor organisms that became major in response to greater light, stronger radiation. The Clouding didn't save these lives. It barely saved ours. So many died in the first decade, when supplements were still in development and architecture unfinished. A long winter before solar heat began at last to radiate from the towers, melting the ice and making the world—such as the Coalition had made it—inhabitable again.

This history informs my designs. I look out into the darkness and imagine homes taking their places between extinct trees, bark shed long ago to expose naked trunks. Mushrooms beneath my feet, soft walls under my fingers. The buildings I make are sculpted to suit the landscape—not in image, so little seen in darkness—but in shape.

I've designed homes that welcome you with fragrant smoke wafting from the senselens by the door. I've designed blocks of apartments, each with its own aroma chosen by clients I've never seen. Smell is the most important aspect of the places I make. Some clients want houses filled with artificialights, but it's illegal to put lights on the outside, disrupting our manufactured darkness. The best way to distinguish a place from without is by smell or sound.

Sound, too, is regulated. Music cannot be played too loud, or too long. We all navigate using our finer senses and intrusions must be kept to a minimum. The world before the Clouding had been bright, loud, polluted with visual and aural stimuli. I can't imagine living in such a place. When the Coalition dissolved and the United Governments constructed humanity's future, a new order began. Quieter—safer.

Scattered insects chirp around me as I walk. I listen to their chorus, the only noise in the dead forest, save for a far-off whining, like an engine in distress. I slow, but the sound dissipates. Whatever it was has stopped or grown too distant to discern. A toad croaks to my left. I return to my normal pace.

While I sometimes incorporate sounds into my designs, I prefer scents. They're nuanced, evocative, personal. My clients give me portfolios of their pasts, presents, futures. Occupations, regional origins, and sensual tastes help me develop the perfect profile for their new home. I use senselenses to blend scents inherited from previous residences with those that signify change. Every aroma is an invisible footprint, a collage of experience and idealism. My own place ...

A branch snaps and I stop. Imagined sensations fade from my mind, leaving a void in its wake. I think for a moment that I smell smoke. Standing still, I scan the ghostly trees.

Shadows and bacterial light. I listen for more noise, but

the forest remains quiet. People rarely veer from the humming path. It's unlikely someone would get lost, but a child might, for a time. Only yesterday, there'd been a story on the news about a transport crash on the other side of the forest. I try to recall what the audio report had said about survivors. I'd been listening to it while working, so my attention had been divided.

I think everyone was found. I think everyone was alright. I don't remember the cause.

I gaze at the dead shapes of trees around me, starved of the light that once let them grow. Nothing moves between them —animal or otherwise. At the end of the work period, in this corner of the forest, I am alone. The mushroom-coated ground luminesces in silent pulses as spores are released. Brief flashes of green reassure me all is well.

I flex my tired fingers, feeling the clay model of the complex I was working on. Luxury apartments, sprawling and spacious. They likely won't be built anywhere near here. Many consider this forest depressing, with its memories of an extinct world.

I find it evocative.

It's a symbol of what we lost, but also what we gained. An abandoned part of the world blended with human innovation. It's everything that stands for us. Our innovation and survival, our destruction and mistakes. The endurance of the natural world, despite it all.

I can imagine these dead trees integrated into a home that smells of soil and warm marble. I've sculpted it many times— only to peel the clay pieces apart when a contract comes in for a building that will actually rise. My idle dreams are just that: dreams.

Unless something changes, I'll never be able to afford a custom home for myself.

My feet tingle with the path's constant vibration, bringing

me back to the present. With a final scan of the fungi-filled forest, I dismiss the broken branch as a product of rot finally winning out. While many trees still stand despite their death, the ground is steadily becoming a graveyard of fallen limbs, eagerly colonized by mushrooms.

My nerves settle and I start walking again, kicking up swirls of light. I turn my thoughts to getting home, closing myself into the dark inside, where the only difference between opening and closing my eyes is sleep.

I increase my pace, looking forward to a quick wash and the soft embrace of my bed to ease my aching back. My gaze sweeps the blackness beyond the path, echoes of my imagination lingering outside the reach of bacterial light. The faint smell of smoke still dogs my steps. I'm beginning to wonder if the engine I heard was the cause … when something flickers.

I slow, staring at the space. A light, caught between one tree shadow and the next. As I move forward, it reappears.

Not blue, like the path. Nor the green of the mushrooms, which have gone dark now. The faint light in the forest is pink.

There are no settlements along the path between the BioHomes unit and my apartment. Besides, artificialights are white, not pink. I stare at the point, thinking maybe it's a new kind of mushroom I haven't seen before. As I watch, it shrinks, and disappears.

I realize that I've stopped. The path vibrates beneath me. I start walking again.

Something rustles. I stop, my pulse spiking. Scanning the darkness, I see it: pink. It's not static, but moving. Bobbing irregularly, changing shape. Getting closer.

Breath in my throat, I step off the path, retreating into familiar darkness. I strain to smell the thing in the trees. I hear it moving, crushing long-dead twigs under it as it lurches towards the blue luminescence of the path. I duck behind a dead trunk.

The pink falters again, vanishing. I hear the thing collapse on the other side of the path. I breathe out.

Besides the soft glow of the bacteria, all is dark. I listen, but I don't hear anything more. What was it I saw? Someone with a pad, screen shining pink? That must have been it. I was being stupid, thinking it was anything more. Just someone walking off the path. Unusual, but not unheard of.

And the thump?

Pulse thrumming in my ears, I step back onto the path. Bacteria ripple around my feet, waves of light reacting to my intrusion. I reach into my pocket, wrapping my fingers around my portable artificialight. I fix my gaze on the place where the pink vanished. *Just someone with a pad, walking where they shouldn't. They must've tripped.*

As I search the darkness, I glimpse it—the faintest flicker.

Like a cut, I think suddenly. *Weeping light instead of blood.*

Gripping my artificialight, I approach the thing. The ground is soft and moist, mushrooms breaking between my toes. The pink lies a few meters from the path, beyond the reach of the little light the bacteria produce.

When I near it, I see it's not a cut, or a mushroom, or a pad. It's a ... a ...

Teeth. Pink, glowing ... *teeth.*

They're framed by ragged lips, chapped skin silhouetted. I draw a breath through my nose, fighting the urge to run back to the path. I smell sickness, dirt, and heat. The scents seem almost familiar, though I'm sure I've never smelled something like this before. It must be ...

A raspy breath slides between unnatural teeth. I step back. The lips move. Another breath.

I open my mouth. I'm not sure whether to talk or scream or breathe. I should just pull out the artificialight, get a fuller picture of this person ... but the thought of the pain, the disorientation the light causes after hours of darkness—

"... clay."

I jerk back, tugging the artificialight from my pocket. Their voice is rough, strained. I clutch the light, pointing it at them but leaving it off, for now. I can see enough, just so long as they stay lying down. "What did you say?"

The glowing teeth twitch. Together, apart. "You smell ... like clay."

I stare at them. "You smell sick." And burned. *Like smoked meat.* The thought is horrible.

They cough, pink light shuddering in the dark. Their breath smells rotten. I back away, retreating closer to the familiar humming of the path.

"Wait!"

I hear them struggling to get up. I hold out my artificialight, finger poised on the switch, though my hand shakes. "Stay there."

They stop moving. Pink teeth face me. I can't see their eyes —it's too dark.

"As if I have a choice."

Their aroma is overpowering, growing stronger the more they talk, the more I linger. Bad skin, I think. Scorched by something. Bad diet too. I wonder how long since they've had access to supplements. An unwelcome feeling creeps through me. My finger slides from the artificialight switch. "You're hurt?"

"Yes." They cough again. Drops of spit reflect the light of their teeth.

I lower the artificialight, but don't return it to my pocket. I could do more damage by exposing them to the beam, especially if they're as weak and disoriented as they seem. Still, they could mean me harm, even in this state. I wish I had more to defend myself than a single light. All my carving tools are in my apartment, still several minutes' walk away.

"Do you"—I suppress nausea; their stench is as concentrated as if it were produced by a senselens—"have a place to go?"

Teeth swing side to side, leaving light echoes in their wake. I swallow. Unusual, for them to use a visual gesture. They're relying on their luminous teeth, it seems, to speak for them. My mouth is dry when I say, "How ... how did you get like this?"

"Bad choices. Not mine."

"Your teeth." I feel like I shouldn't mention it, but I can't stop staring. Nothing living glows. *Except bacteria, and fungi, of course*. Could that be it? Some sort of infection? But ... on teeth? Still, maybe it's a clue to what happened to them. "I've ... I've never seen anything like that."

They smile, illuminating the space between us. Now I see their body—covered in cuts and welts. Their clothes are half burned away. The rest of their face remains dark. "I'm lucky to still have them. Most of us lose them to radiation."

My throat tightens. "Radiation? Where?" There haven't been issues with radiation poisoning since the Clouding. Has something gone wrong? Have the clouds grown thin?

"Everywhere," they say. "Even at night."

I stare at them. The prickling sense of dread that's been growing under my skin spreads up my neck, down my arms. "There's no night. No day. Just now."

They cough, a rending sound. "That's what they tell you."

Anger flares in me, muffling my fear. "It's the truth."

"Down here, maybe. For now."

They lurch to their feet faster than I thought possible, the aura of sickness pouring from their skin. I back up, but not quicky enough. Their hand finds my wrist, seizing me. I drop the artificialight. Their palm is rough with blisters. I feel their breath on my face, pink teeth piercing my eyes.

I gasp, choking on their scent. When I see their face—or what remains of it—bile sears my throat.

They have no eyes. Above their mouth, the flesh is twisted, burned and scarred in ripples over their skull. They have no hair.

"*Above* the clouds, though"—they gasp, leaning against me—"we burn."

I try to hold my breath, backing up, seeking the subtle humming of the path. Whoever this person is, they're unwell. Something has happened to them, and they're confused. Angry. Sick. Very sick.

I try to keep my voice calm, my face turned away from that awful glowing mouth. "There's nothing above the clouds. Only the towers, with the spinners. It's all automated. Besides ... no one could survive up there."

I believe what I'm saying, I think. Yes. It's history. It's fact.

My heel finds the edge of the path. Blue light swarms around our feet. Of course, they can't see it. I wonder if they can feel the vibrations in the air.

When I look at them, I find a pink glowing smile. Their voice rasps in my ear, burned and broken.

"I did."

THEY CAN'T SEE the path, but they must be able to feel it. They drag me a few meters along it, and then whatever's destroying their body triumphs, and they collapse again. I stand beside them, shaking from more than the vibrations under my feet. Seeing them now in the light of the bacteria, they're horrible. Covered in sores and scars, twisted and thin, nearly naked. What clothes they have are scorched and torn, stained with blood and worse. They might once have been denim or heavy canvas. The kind of clothes you wear for industrial work.

They look ... they look like history. They look like the

photos, videos, and accounts of the time before the Clouding. They look like medical journals and government records.

They look like apocalypse.

No. It's not true. It can't be. I try to think of alternate explanations for their condition—rare diseases, lack of supplements, even self-harm. Some chemical explosion, maybe. I remember the story about the transport crash, not far from here. My muddled brain latches onto it, though the details remain fuzzy. Maybe they were involved. That could account for the burns and cuts, and now I discern something else in their scent to back up this theory: engine oil.

Okay, a crash victim, maybe confused. That at least presents me with a clear course of action: I should bring them to the hospital.

Coughs shake them, the light from their exposed teeth mixing with bacterial luminescence to form a purple glow. My half-formed explanations disperse. No matter what I conjure, I can't ignore their teeth, or the other smells.

In the face of more reasonable explanations, I find myself wondering: how many cancers stir under their skin? If they've spent years above the clouds ...

It's impossible. A lie.

"Can you walk?"

They stop coughing, heaving against the path. A sore on their cheek weeps shimmering pus. "That depends."

"On?"

"Where you want me to walk."

I swallow. They reek worse than the most pungent mushrooms. Against my better judgement, I say, "I live a little ways from here. Along the path." *I should bring them to the hospital, not home.*

They turn their head, cheek quivering against the path, breathing through their mouth. *Could a hospital even help them, at this point?*

"If I get found, I'll be killed."

My breath hitches. "Who's looking for you?"

They push themselves up onto their melted knees. Bacteria swirls around their cuts. "The Coalition."

What? "No."

The Coalition dissolved eighty years ago. We owe our world to them. We owe our lives.

I try to explain, unnerved by the quivering uncertainty in my voice. "You must've been in a crash. That's what made you like this. You're … confused. Hurt. I can get you help." Behind my reasoning, something else whispers: *But the smell. They smell like fire. And worse.*

They smile at me, bitter and pink. "I *was* in a crash."

I breathe out. At last, a real reason for the way they look. A crash explains the smell, too. *And the teeth?* I push the thought away. "I can help you, bring you to the hospital. There's a transport station on the other side of the woods, if you can walk that far." I hope they can walk on their own. I don't really want to touch them again. "Do you have a name?"

Teeth face me. "Do you?"

I open my mouth, my brief spell of sense unspooling. I realize I would never ask someone that question if I believed … but what they're saying is insane.

I try to keep a hold on myself. The dark is suddenly oppressive, the humming of the path too loud. I don't want to stay here, where anyone might come along and find us. Find *them*, looking the way they do. "Of course I have a name."

"Then why shouldn't I?"

My stomach churns from more than the stench. "Mallory. I'm Mallory."

They grimace. Or maybe it's a smile.

"Rein."

Unease wins out against disgust. I reach down and take one of Rein's ruined hands, pulling them up to their feet.

Scabs scrape my palm and I almost let go. *They need help*, I tell myself. I hold on. "I'm sorry. I just—this way."

I start walking, guiding them along the path through the dead woods. It's late. We shouldn't run into anyone else, if we're lucky. *If I'm lucky.*

Rein keeps up, walking more or less on their own, as I'd hoped. In front of them, their smell is less oppressive. I breathe deep, trying to make sense of the last ten minutes of my life.

Yesterday, wasn't it? That's when the transport crashed. News said no survivors, but maybe they missed one. Rein was pretty far from the reported crash site. Unable to see, they must've wandered in the wrong direction.

But even that didn't make sense. We're all used to darkness. Even without eyes, they should have known the way. They should have sensed the right direction.

Those scars are old. They've been blind for a long time. And what caused it? I look over my shoulder at them. So thin. What they need most is water, and food. The hospital will have that.

Their words replay in my head: *If I get found, I'll be killed.* They were lying, right? Paranoid, maybe. Another symptom of trauma. I try to remember the cause of the transport crash. Was it pilot error? Sensor malfunction? The path vibrates under my feet. We're still a long way from the station.

At a familiar bend, I smell home. I make a decision I fear I'll regret.

I veer off the path, drawing Rein with me. They falter, pulling back on my hand. "Where are we going?"

I'm asking myself a slightly different question: *What am I doing?* "My home. Do you smell it?"

They open their glowing mouth. After a moment, they smile. "Clay."

"I'm a designer," I explain, realizing I don't expect them to understand. As if they're not from this world—*my* world. "I make clay models of buildings, and people pay my company to build them."

Rein nods, their teeth rising and falling in the dark. "We used clay. Not for building—I don't think."

The confusion in their voice helps convince me they're disoriented. Maybe they were in the transport crash after all. Before then they must've been ill. Maybe they were on their way to a hospital. Lack of supplements, some sort of explosion. Combine it all, and it makes sense.

Except I'm not bringing them to the hospital. I'm bringing them home. If I believe the truth is so simple, why am I trying to hide them, instead of getting real help?

"I'm surprised," Rein says, stumbling behind me. "That you'd use up your final hours like this."

"What?" I glance at them again. They're too young to have lived before the Clouding. I think they're about my age, but their body is frail, like a pencil sharpened all the way down to the end.

They turn their teeth towards me, ignoring my question. "What kind of buildings? Towers?"

"N-no. I make homes."

"Did you make yours?"

"No. I don't—I mean, I live in an apartment."

They say nothing to that. My skin crawls where I hold their hand. I made my choice, though. Unstable or dying, I decided to help them.

I bring them through flourishing mushrooms to my door, the senselens releasing puffs of clay aroma so I can find it easily in the dark. We're far enough from the path that the only light here comes from Rein's teeth.

I feel for the door pad and scan my hand to unlock it. Rein stumbles on the ramp behind me.

"I'm sorry." I guide them through the door, holding onto their scarred forearm. They don't seem used to the design of the doorway, though it's standard. All entrances follow the same dimensions, simple to navigate in darkness.

I try to brush off the implications of their confusion, their smell that becomes nearly overpowering when we're inside. Still holding their arm, I close out the world.

I've never brought someone here before. Usually, I keep my apartment completely dark. It's small, just one room. I know every surface. Even when sculpting models, I prefer darkness. It's what I'm used to.

Now, the light from Rein's teeth illuminates the whole space, reflecting off objects I didn't think reflective. Seeing the smallness is worse than feeling it. Visually, my home is tiny. Hardly a living space. I would never design something so wanting.

I'm glad they can't see what I see.

"Here." I try to gather myself. I guide them to my bed, sitting them down on the rumpled covers. Everything is cast in the raw pink of their glowing.

"Do you want ... something?" I can't decide whether to offer them water or bandages first.

Their fingers quest across the covers, leaving flakes of scab in their wake. My stomach turns at the sight. "This is?" they ask.

"My bed."

"Where you?"

"Sleep?" I don't mean for it to be a question. Rein lowers their head, spreading their hands across the wrinkled sheets. I'll have to wash them once they're ...

Gone? Better? Dead? I don't know.

"Sleep," they echo. Then, "You have a lot of clay here. The smell was so strong."

"My senselens produces a clay scent. It's ... appropriate, I guess you could say, given what I do." I couldn't afford anything more elaborate. Mixed scents are more expensive.

Their mouth turns down. "Senselens?"

I stare at their eyeless face. They must know what a sense-lens is. Every building since the Clouding has been built with at least one at every entrance. *If they don't know about them, then …*

I back away, fighting my worsening nausea. "I have some medical stuff. I can try to patch up your burns."

Rein moves their head in what could be a nod. I take a breath, glad to have some direction. I turn away and navigate half by feel, half by the dim light that slips between their lips. It takes me a few minutes, but I gather everything I need: antiseptic gel, bandages, a bowl of water, and a few cloths. I bring the supplies back to the bed.

"Rein?" They've flopped over, mouth slack. The reek of sickness is strong, overcoming the familiar scent of my sculptures.

Panic surges through me. What do I do if they die? Where do I put them? I don't know how to dispose of a corpse, especially one that's possibly wanted. *Possibly radioactive.* If what they said is true, someone is looking for them. Certainly not the Coalition, but someone. They must be missed.

"Rein?" I set down the bowl of water and touch their skin. It's hotter than it should be, but with no trace of sweat. I cover their mouth with my hand. I can feel their breaths. They're only asleep.

My relief is short-lived. Leaning over them, wondering if a fever is the final, far-fetched explanation for their condition, I see a frayed badge peeling up from their ruined chest. I narrow my eyes, blocking the soft glow of their teeth and waiting for my vision to adjust.

A number is sewn onto their clothes. It's been distorted by burns, but I can read it.

25683-80-774

Cold trickles along my veins. I've worked with number

keys my entire career. This one is simple, unnervingly close to the codes I use for my living.

25683 could spell many words, depending on the cipher, but I've only seen it translated to one: *CLOUD*. And the middle number—80—is self-explanatory. Both numbers have preceded every design I've been assigned over the past year. I've seen them so often, I hardly read them anymore.

Now, my gaze hitches on each digit. *25683-80*. The eightieth year since the Clouding. *774*, though, I don't know. But I have an idea.

Number keys are used to identify and catalog. It's how BioHomes files their constructions, keeps a record of business. This badge is nearly identical in format, but it's not for a building or list of supplies.

It's for a person.

If the uniform—because that's what it must be, burned beyond repair—is an identifier, then Rein is number 774. The seven hundred and seventy-fourth individual, eighty years since the Clouding.

I've run out of shrouds to cover the truth. Rein seems otherworldly because in a way, they are. They're not from the darkness I've known my whole life.

They're from the other side of the clouds.

I DON'T SLEEP. I don't know what I should do, but I'm sure I don't do it.

At first I just stand there, staring at the stranger on my bed. Then I open all the shutters, letting in fresh air. I worry it might also let Rein's reek out, so I program my senselens to a higher output, hoping clay will overpower the scent of ruined flesh to any passersby.

Their number spins in my head, mixing with the

numbers of every design I've sculpted for clients I've never met. 774. Rein. The digits don't match the letters in their name, which means it's not a translation or transcription. The number isn't a reference for their identity; it's a replacement.

A number, a name. I stare at them, more blemish than person. I hold my breath until their chest rises, lets me know that they live—barely.

I flee to my tiny kitchen, hands trembling and mouth dry. Rein's smell follows me. I look for something—anything—to cover it up.

Under the sink, I unearth my small first aid kit, unopened since I moved in six years ago. I tear the plastic in uneven shreds until my sweaty fingers are at last able to pry the tin open. Supplies scatter over my lap and the floor.

Will it be enough?

I expect Rein to wake the moment I touch them, peeling their ruined clothes in pieces from scorched skin, but their breathing—labored and shallow—stays unchanged as I work.

I didn't realize the extent of the damage. Once I begin tending them, I can't stop. I spend hours cleaning and dressing every sore on Rein's body, uncovering new wounds even as I patch the worst. I don't find a single section of unscarred, unbroken skin. Even their inner thighs, the soft flesh of their genitals—all have been tortured by whatever conditions they weathered before stumbling into my sight.

My trepidation at touching them withers almost immediately. Their condition is beyond belief; beyond humanity. Have they ever been treated before? I see the remnants of infections and lumps I fear are cancers spreading under their emaciated muscles. I run out of antiseptic gel and resort to washing them with water, wrapping gauze over almost every part of their wasted body.

When I run out of gauze, I unearth a small box of plastic

bandages in the bathroom cabinet. I stick these across their blisters until I've used them up as well.

Sores remain. I tear up the clean cloths I use in sculpting. Tying them around Rein's raw ankles, I can almost imagine the apocalyptic world above the clouds.

All we know is what earth was like before the Clouding: exposed to the fullness of the sun. Toxic air. Poisonous light. I know the history, but all I've lived is cool, measured. Bioluminescence produces no fire, no burns. Artificialight is bland and sterile.

The closest I can come to picturing the sun are the metal halide lights in greenhouses, coaxing plants to grow and provide food for those who can afford it. I've designed these places, modeled them out of clay. I've seen them—albeit from a distance. I've never been inside, nor tasted the produce they cultivate. My limited income can only afford mushrooms and supplements.

When I run out of the last of my cloths, I sink back onto my knees. Rein is sprawled on my bed, more bandage than body.

The Coalition swore no more people would suffer the sight of the sun. The towers and their spinners are automated. Any maintenance is carried out under the clouds. But it's been eighty years. Maybe ... a fault? Could it be that after almost a century, some towers are wearing out?

Something Rein said hovers in the back of my mind, too vague to grasp. Something about time running out, a final darkness ...

I watch their narrow chest rise and fall. The number on their uniform—now stuffed in my waste bin, buried under soiled towels—might be for work, or something worse. Prisons, I know, went out with the sun. Detention centers have replaced them, serving as holding places before trials determine innocence or guilt. If guilty, the sentence is typically a new name, new location; a new profession designed to prevent repetition of fault.

Surely no one could be sentenced to forced labor. No one could be sent up above the clouds. Even if something was wrong with a tower, such exposure could only lead to death.

Neither possibility sits right with me now, my hands sticky with antiseptic gel and blood.

AN HOUR before I would normally get up, I wash out the bowl and throw the last stained cloths I used to clean Rein's wounds into the bin. My body aches. My head pounds like I've been staring into an artificialight. I should go to bed, get what rest I can, but I can't bring myself to lie down where Rein sprawls. I walk outside instead, closing the door behind me.

I breathe, emptying my lungs of the sickness that fills my apartment. Outside, I can almost convince myself that nothing has changed. The forest is backlit by fungal emissions, ghostly green in the dark. I look from tree to listing tree, emptying my mind of the wrongness on the other side of my door. Instead, I imagine a house nestled between the bare trunks.

Over the years, I've often pictured the home that might one day hold me. I know its curves and smells, the texture of the floor. But I know too that it will never be mine.

I can't afford my own designs. I can't afford the rates BioHomes charge clients for my models. Clay scent wafts around me, imperfectly concealing other odors. I rub my wrist, sorer now than before. My skin is tacky with antiseptic, dried pus trapped under my nails.

Indecision grips me with icy hands. Do I leave now? Do I call for an emergency transport to take Rein to the hospital? Do I walk to BioHomes and call the authorities?

If I get found, I'll be killed.

Rein's words throw me into a deeper spiral. I mean to run, but I don't make it more than a few steps from my door. Exhausted, I stumble through a dense row of mushrooms and sink to my knees. What do I know, anyway? What can I do?

In a fairy circle, I curl up on the ground. I fall asleep in total darkness.

———

WHEN I AWAKE, a light is shining in my face. I smell poison.

"Mallory. Mallory, please."

Rein's voice is rough, unfamiliar. I blink at their twisted, eyeless face. Their teeth glow mercilessly.

They're so close to my nightmares, shouldering false terrors away to replace them with real ones. I roll to one side, feeling sick. Mushrooms split under me, wet and cold. I remember where I am, what I've done. Can I catch what they carry? I stare at my hands, stained red in the pink light of their teeth. No sores, yet.

"You left me." Rein's tone is strained. Before, they sounded accusing, abrasive. Their voice is different now. I realize the subtle change is fear. They're afraid.

"I—" Post-rest clarity is brutal. I should never have brought them into my home. I should never have touched them, told them my name. I push myself up to my knees, listening. Staying outside was just one in a string of bad choices.

"Come on." I take their bandaged hand and hurry back inside, dragging Rein through the clay-scented cloud produced by my senselens. My pulse is running. It begins to dawn on me just how royally fucked I might be.

"You did this?"

Trying not to hyperventilate, I look at Rein, their teeth illuminating the air between us. They hold up their arms, touching the bandages I wrapped over their burns.

"While you were sleeping." I realize now how creepy that was. They're still naked, except for the sections of gauze and cloth I wrapped around their wounds. "Uh. Hope that was okay."

They run their fingers over the gauze, swaying, their breaths raspy. "It feels ... I feel ... cool."

I catch them just in time. They're surprisingly light, more than I noticed when I moved them around to bandage them. I help them back to my bed, letting them sit with their back against the wall.

Fears and questions clamor in my head. I wish I knew how to approach them, but all I can do is look at Rein's eyeless face, their skin covered in bandages that have already started to stain. My limited treatment is as effective as a sponge trying to mop up the sea.

I try to organize my still sleep-muddled thoughts. "You need to eat something. Drink water."

I leave them gasping and fill a pitcher from my pump, pouring them a glass. In the face of a growing headache, I fill one for me too. I cross my tiny home back to Rein, lifting their hand and folding their fingers around the glass. "Here."

Uncertain, they take a sip. Their teeth shine through the water, ripples of light finding the cracks between their fingers. Not trusting them to keep a solid grip on the glass, I support it from the bottom, taking a sip from my own in my other hand.

They cough, and I take the glass back. If there's a chance of catching something from them, I think I've caught it by now. "Careful."

They run their tongue over their scarred lips. "Water?"

"Yes. Is it okay?"

"It's cold."

"I can make it warmer ..."

"No!" They reach out blindly, finding the glass and taking it back, in both hands this time. I perch on the edge of the bed, unsure. I haven't been sure of anything since I saw those teeth, shining pink between dead trees.

Rein gulps the water, emptying the glass and holding it against their bandaged chest. "It feels ... good. It hurts less."

"I'm sorry. That you hurt, I mean."

They smile, lips cracking. "We're used to it."

"When—" I stop, try again. Everything feels like the wrong thing to say. "How long were you there—above the clouds? When did you start?"

They face me, incomplete expression unreadable. Anger slides back into their tone. "Years. Before that—it wasn't much better." Their expression sharpens. "They lied to us. All of it—*lies.*"

"Did you see ..." I can't stop looking at where their eyes used to be.

Rein holds their glass out, a physical intrusion on the answer to my unfinished question. "More?"

I hand them my water, cradling their empty glass in my lap. They swallow, pink-tinged water dripping from their chin. At length, they say, "You mean the sun." There's less venom in their voice.

My mouth is dry despite the water I just drank. Sometime between falling asleep outside and waking to their teeth, I committed myself to their truth.

I see their number in my head, a black scar on twisted fabric.

"Yes."

They lean their head against the wall. "Imagine everything exposed. Imagine air that burns your skin. Imagine the glare of fire on white clouds." They pause, licking their lips. "I was glad when my eyes melted away. I was happy not to feel it anymore."

The image hangs between us. I have no words.

"It can almost be beautiful," Rein says softly, "when the sun sets, and the stars bring a few hours of relief. But this ..." Their fingers crawl over the lip of the glass, running through what drops remain at the bottom. "I couldn't have imagined it."

Silence fills the apartment. My headache is worsening. After a few minutes, Rein lifts their head. "Describe it to me."

"What?"

"Here."

I stare at them, teeth the only light. "Do you mean my apartment, or the world?"

"Both. Either."

"It's ..." How do I start? My life seems so little. I search for images they could understand, some sense to compare to nonsense. "We don't rely on sight. I know the feel of everything I own. I never use light unless I need something I can't find by my other senses. I make models with clay and write up the measurements on lightless pads, or with a very soft light that won't disrupt my senses. Outside ...

"The land is a mix of before and now. Most plants died. Some are kept alive with artificial lights. Many of the wild plants are fungi. I've ... I've never seen what most of the world looks like in light. I've grown up under the clouds."

"I think I felt them—the mushrooms." Rein rubs the tips of their fingers together, lips downturned. "They were cold."

"They're in the woods, where I found you."

Their frown deepens. "And that path?"

"It vibrates to activate bacteria that bioluminesce. They generate a little light so people can find the paths that connect settlements."

Rein nods. Their movements tell me they're used to being

seen. Even without eyes, they are adapted to operating where others take visual cues.

"Above," I swallow. Time feels delicate, here. "What are the people like?"

Rein's hands return to their glass, tightening. "Dying."

"You escaped?"

They nod, lips pressed together. Their teeth glow ghostly on the other side, illuminating the shadows of veins and skin.

"How?" I ask.

Their hands release the glass, move to pick at the bandages on their legs. "You must be expected somewhere. When?"

There it is: our moment of unreality is broken. Stories can't fix this. Words won't put my life back to where it was twelve hours ago.

"I work here," I say. "Sometimes I tour a development site. Yesterday I was working in the office. I was on my way back when I found you." I stand and pick up my scheduling pad, running my fingers over the raised dates. "I have forty-eight hours before I need to go back in."

Rein coughs. I take their glass, refilling it and mine from the pitcher. Again, I hear my pulse in my ears. "I can stay, look after you."

"I can't stay, Mallory."

Their tone is strained from more than sickness. I bring the glasses back to the bed. Their teeth shimmer. Something from another world, I think again—but it's not, is it? It's *my* world, and I should know about it. Everyone should know about it.

"Why were you up there?" I ask.

Rein takes the glass I offer. They dip their fingers in, stirring slowly. "The Coalition collected us, promised it would be better. But it was all lies. We weren't fixing anything. Only breaking it, breaking our bodies for them to hide a little longer." Water drips down their arm. I worry it'll loosen the bandages, make the plasters unstick. It's a stupid, little fear. But it's an easier one to face.

Rein stops stirring, teeth gritting together. "They need us. But we know the truth, now. One way or another ..." They turn towards me. "I escaped, but I didn't vanish. They're going to be looking for me."

"The Coalition." The word is changed when Rein says it. It used to mean salvation. It used to be a glorious figure in history. Now it tastes burned in my mouth.

Rein reaches out. Not sure what they want, I take their hand. Their grip is tighter than I expected. "You found me, and helped me. I don't know why. You can see I'm dying. I should've died in the crash. And you ..." Their mouth quivers. "Take the time you have left and stay out of this."

Time left? "I don't understand," I say, my hand warming in their grip. "The Coalition disintegrated after the Clouding. Why were you up there? Why would they come after you now?"

Rein's smile is like a gash. "I'm alive. I'm here—on the wrong side of the clouds. The Coalition has to kill me."

"But—"

"There's nothing you can do, Mallory. If they find me here, I don't know what will happen to you. They'll want to know what you know about me and the rebellion."

"*Rebellion?*" The dread that's been stirring in me rises, making my throat tight.

Rein releases my hand at last. My palm is smeared with congealed blood and gel. "There are others," they say. "There will be more."

"More ... more like you? From above?"

"As many as possible. You don't have any idea what you involved yourself in when you helped me. You can't keep me here. They *will* find me."

I stare at their twisted skin. As horrible as it is, Rein's

right. There's nothing more I can do for them. A treacherous relief fills me. They'll be gone; my life will be back to how it was. How it should be. "Where will you go?"

They put the glass to their broken lips and drink for a long time. When they finish, and still say nothing, I realize that's it.

Rein doesn't know where to go. This side of the clouds is as alien to them as their side is to me.

But they always knew this world existed. No one here—no one I know, at least—has any idea people work above the clouds. We were never told.

How many are there like Rein? I see their number in my mind again. 774. Seven hundred others, at least. Alive? Dead? Or in between, like Rein is—close to burning away.

But if something like that was going on, if people were coming down from the clouds ... wouldn't there be news? Confusion, outrage? It doesn't make sense.

Then the other things they said begin to hit me. *Final hours. Time you have left.* I no longer feel any relief at the idea of Rein leaving. Their presence is a warning of more than injustice.

Mind buzzing, I get up and go to the kitchen. I offer Rein food—some stewed mushrooms with dissolved supplements —and they take it without speaking. I know I should have something too, but nausea prevents me. Instead I watch them eat, listening for someone outside, fearing the sound of knocking. Standing in the middle of my claustrophobic apartment, prying blood from under my nails, I inhale stale air heavy with the scent of sickness and clay.

Clay.

I look at Rein. Despite their conviction, they're asleep again, empty bowl in their bandaged lap. I sit down at my desk. Running my hands across the mat, I pick up a clump of unmolded clay.

In the dark, I begin to sculpt.

I'VE ALMOST FINISHED when my pad pings three low tones, startling the tools from my fingers. I tap the answer key. I know from the ring that it's Jayde, my supervisor.

"Hi, Jayde." I hope my voice sounds normal. I certainly don't feel normal, soft pink reflecting off my ceiling as Rein sleeps in my bed.

"Mallory. How are those new designs coming along?"

I try to remember what I was working on yesterday. It feels like a century away, or maybe just eighty years. It was a big contract. Something ... ah, yes. The luxury apartment complex, each room perfumed to evoke a different region. Simply walking from one to the next would be like traveling the world.

"In the final stages," I say, groping along my desk until my fingers find the corner of one finished model. "I sent you digitals of the main structure, and I'll be designing the interiors this week. They'll be ready for the showing in June."

"Good. BioHomes is relying on this contract to round off the quarter. By the way, that complex on the other side of the forest is almost ready for touring. There's a launch next week, if you want to be there. Not many of the locations end up being local to you. You deserve to sense a finished product."

The complex? My mind whirls. Yes—it was designed nearly a year ago. A sprawling multi-generation home, integrating the dead trees into the lines of the architecture. A project that I truly enjoyed. I have so few chances to incorporate a setting I know, and this one I walk weekly. The clients requested sense-lenses all along the outer walls, releasing puffs of ... what was it?

"Mallory?" Jayde's voice jerks me back.

"Yes. Thanks, Jayde. I'd love to be there."

"Good. I look forward to feeling those new designs."

The call clicks off. I exhale. *Water.* That's what the clients wanted for the senselenses. The smell of fresh, cool water to welcome them home. I get up and go to the sink, pouring myself a glass, inhaling its soft scent. When I return to my desk, two eyes are staring at me. I can just make out the lines I scored in faint pink light.

Under artificialight, no one will believe they're real. But in darkness, with only the softness of bioluminescence, they're the best I can think of. *And if the complex in the woods is finished, empty…*

I drink my water and set the glass down, following the scent of decay to Rein's body, their teeth a strip of unnatural light splitting their mouth in two.

"Rein?"

I'm surprised they slept through my call with Jayde. The fear that they've died returns to me, and I shake them, flinching at the heat that seems to kindle under their burned skin, only slightly muffled by bandages. Their breath hitches and their lips move.

"They'll find me."

"No one saw us on the path." I'm certain we were alone then. When we were outside the apartment, I'm not so sure. My senselens should have muffled Rein's scent, at least.

They cough. "The Coalition can track radiation. I'm like a shining light in the darkness. They'll find me."

I exhale, an unfamiliar thrill of impulsiveness running through me. No time to come up with something better. *My plan it is.* I take their bandaged hands. "I know a place we can go. But I need to change the way you look. Is that okay?"

Rein's mouth twists, blisters reforming into a raw smile. They tug one hand back, running their fingers over the melted skin of their face. "It makes no difference to me."

I swallow. It feels rude, staring at their injury. But I can't look away. The scars are becoming familiar. "Okay. Come here."

I lead them across my apartment and sit them in the chair at my desk. I pick up an unformed lump of clay and put it in their hands.

"Clay," they say, putting it to their mutilated nose.

"I've made you … false eyes. And covers, for your teeth. No one glows like that here. It might make it hard for you to talk, at least until we get to where we're going."

They press their fingers into the clay I gave them, leaving imprints. "Won't people see it's fake?"

"Not in the dark." *I hope.* My heart thrums in my chest.

Rein runs their tongue over their lips. "Are you sure you want to do this?"

"Yes." I'm surprised at my lack of hesitation. They face me, chin upturned.

"Why?"

I open my mouth. Is it guilt? Pity? They're dying; I can see that, despite my medical ignorance. They need skin grafts, chemotherapy, and antibiotics to at least have a chance, and I have none of those. All I can do is lead them to another hiding place. Whether I succeed or not, they won't last long. It's pointless to even try.

"Because you escaped," I say. "And the world needs to know what you saw—I mean, what you lived."

Eyeless, I can't tell their expression. After a moment, they nod. "Okay."

In silence I commit to my latest rash decision. I take the clay from their hands and begin molding it over their face, smoothing out their scars. I turn their ruined face into a blank model, and onto it I add the eyes I've made, carefully pressing them into place. I carve eyebrows, add clay to their nose to give it the right shape. When I've finished, Rein wears a clay mask.

I step back, gazing at them in the light of their teeth. I

wonder if I've got it right. Was this what they looked like before? Was this how they grew up—if they grew up at all, if they had a chance to live before someone put them on the wrong side of the clouds?

"Well?"

I wish I could show them. "You look good," I tell them. They snort. It's short, but feels like the most intimate noise. Part of a self that was hidden until now.

"I bet. What about this muzzle you made?"

I pick up the last two pieces of clay, molded into crescents to cover Rein's glowing teeth. I place them in their hands. "You can put them in yourself. They should conform to your teeth."

Rein runs their fingers along the pieces. They settle one over their lower teeth, the other over the top. We're dropped into darkness.

"Tashtsh like dirt," they observe. I giggle, despite myself. Despite the situation.

"Sorry. Nothing is that color here. It would've given you away."

"Mallory ..."

"Rein." Saying their name feels almost like a transgression. Acknowledging their selfhood means acknowledging their reality. And with it, my last chance to turn away.

"Thanksh. You didn't ... you don't have to do thish."

I feel them in front of me, their breaths brushing my skin. In darkness, I can imagine they're like me. I can imagine they've lived a better life. I swallow, their scent betraying the lie. "Come on."

It's almost easier finding my way through the apartment in customary darkness. I lead Rein to my closet and get them dressed in my clothes. I should change what I'm wearing—I've lost track of how long it's been—but I don't know how much time we have. As soon as Rein is dressed, most of the bandages covered and a hood up to help hide their false face, we go outside.

The air is cool and damp. It smells like rain.

I lead Rein through the mushrooms and up onto the vibrating path. We walk side by side. I don't sense anyone nearby, but this is the main route through the forest. To hope we can make it through a second time without running into another person borders on stupidity.

"Where are you taking me?" Rein whispers, voice hoarse. They sound muffled and slurred with clay over their teeth. Like they're on the other side of a wall, with no door to connect us.

"There's a complex on the other side of the forest," I say, keeping my gaze fixed on the path ahead. I want to have as much warning as possible if someone's coming the other way. "I designed it for my company about a year ago. It's been built, and it won't be occupied until next week. I know the floor plan, how to get in and out. The clients will change the settings when they move in, but for now everything will be on default."

"It won't help. They'll jusht follow."

I think I hear something. I stop, Rein stopping with me. After several tense seconds, I figure I must've imagined it. I drop my voice lower.

"It buys time, at least. We can figure out what to do after that."

"We?"

I open my mouth, but I smell something now. Someone is on the path, the breeze carrying their scent to me. I tighten my grip on Rein's arm.

"Someone's coming."

We can't stop. Standing still on the path, with nothing around but dead trees, is suspicious on its own. I try to keep our walking regular. I don't see any light ahead, which means whoever's coming doesn't have an artificialight, or at least isn't using it. Small luck.

I hear them now: footsteps on the path. A few more seconds, and I see a dim shape lit by the soft blue of the bacteria. I hold onto Rein as if my grip alone can protect them from detection.

The person smells of oil. They probably work on machinery, maybe the same works that comprise the path under us. I meet their eyes as we pass, exchanging a polite nod. They glance at Rein, nose wrinkling. They step off the path to go around us.

I hold my breath until I can't hear their steps anymore. When I exhale, Rein turns their head towards me.

"They shmelled like the cloud controlsh."

"Cloud controls? Are those part of the machines that make the clouds—the spinners?" We never learned much about them. History focuses on the result: the towers hold the spinners, the spinners make clouds, the clouds stop the sun. We survive.

Rein bobbles their head. "Short of. Coalition work them, with protection. Shuitsh that block the raysh. But the machinesh are oursh."

They work the spinners. But the towers were supposed to be automated. No one was meant to work them, once they were built.

Was it always a lie? Or did something change?

I try to keep both my pace and voice level. "What do you do?"

"Make repairsh. Clean debris out of the fansh. And shometimesh—"

My pulse jumps as I glimpse silhouettes ahead. "Someone else is coming."

Again, no artificialight. I try to control my breathing as two people, moving single file, pass us on the path. They smell of soil. They likely work in agriculture, harvesting mushrooms or subterranean animals for consumption. They pass on my side now, and I'm grateful neither looks closely at Rein.

I glance at Rein. Their eyes stare blindly ahead, clay tinged blue by activated bacteria. Their teeth are neutered gray. "What happens sometimes?" I ask them when I think the couple is far enough away.

"What?"

"What you were saying. You repair the machines, clean them. And sometimes—?"

They run their tongue over their lips, clay. "People fall."

"Fall? Wait, like ... through the clouds?"

"Through machinesh. Crushed, then fall."

"Down here?"

Rein shrugs. "I think. I bet they're cleaned away. Hidden in the dark."

"But ... someone must notice if—if *pieces* of people are falling through the clouds!"

"Radiation tracking," Rein murmurs. "From the chemicalsh they give ush. Easy to find."

I stare at Rein's face. My clay additions no longer seem merely strange. It would be so easy to smudge the illusion, peel the pieces away. I imagine their real eyes and skin slipping through gears, shredded and scattered through the clouds to feed the growth of mushrooms.

I wonder how much I've brushed against in the dark, stepped through on my way to and from my normal life, worrying about the dimensions of homes I'll never see. When I look around, I don't see a forest of trees, pale and barkless in the dark. I see a catacomb of bare bones.

The path vibrates with a sudden pulse, numbing my feet. Rein stumbles.

"What'sh that?"

"I don't know." I've never felt something like this. The

pulse comes again, creeping up on us and then sliding past. A third comes, the delay between them shorter than before.

Distantly, I hear an engine. Rein's arm stiffens in my grasp as a fourth pulse thrums under us and stays. It dogs our uneven steps.

"Off the path," they gasp. "Get me off!"

They lurch away, dragging us down onto the mushroom-strewn ground. Behind us, the path's glow brightens like a beacon, concentrated around the space we walked a moment before.

My breath knots in my chest. "How did—that's not what the bacteria do!"

"I told you," Rein hisses, head swinging from side to side, free arm groping through the dead trees. "I told you they'd find me."

"But the path—" I never imagined the technology could be bent like that, used for tracking. Had it always had that capability? Every trip I've made through the forest, tired and distracted, complacent in my thoughts ...

All that time, had I been subject to scans checking my chemical signal, reading my identity through the soles of my feet?

The engine sound is no longer distant. It's a transport motoring over the forest, homing in on the area where Rein dragged us from the path.

"How much longer?" they ask, pulling me blindly away from the sound. "Which way?"

I try to remember the coordinates. Without the path to guide me, I'm almost as lost as they are. I slide my arm around their back, trying to wipe my mind of panic as the transport roars behind us. There will be a time to reexamine my life (maybe). Now, I need to focus on Rein's chances.

"We're close," I say. I hope I'm right. I charge through the trees, tripping over sticks and wishing for the light of Rein's teeth to give me a little guidance. The humming transport—thankfully not getting closer—assures me that any light now would surely expose us.

Path to our right, I guide Rein as best I can through the dark. I visited the site where the complex was to be built a year ago. I measured it, decided which dead trees needed removal, and which would be coated with resin and preserved to provide aesthetics. I haven't been to the area since.

The path forks, curving away and plunging us into greater darkness. I can still hear the transport, though it doesn't seem to be following—which is a temporary relief. The trees thicken around us, and I'm comforted by the notion that we're unlikely to meet anyone else travelling off the path.

Just when I'm getting nervous that I misremembered, leading us into endless dead woods, I smell it: water.

The aroma hits us in a wave as we enter the property lines. I remember being hesitant about the quantity of senselenses the clients requested, and the scent is truly overpowering.

The vapor is thick enough to block even the noxious odor of Rein beside me. I feel like I'm drowning.

"What ..." Rein gags. I drag them towards the complex, following the ripples of scent produced by the senselenses. I can't hear the transport anymore. We made it.

"It's just the senselenses," I tell them, gasping. I never realized senselenses could be this powerful. I've never designed a place with so many. The most I've ever encountered around an entrance is four. This complex has eight. "It'll be better—" I draw a labored breath. "—inside."

I find the wall with my outstretched free hand and follow it to the door. I use the default code associated with my design profile, hoping the clients didn't request an early change. It works. I shove the door open and haul Rein inside, locking the water scent outside. Within, I can breathe with only a slight aroma, cool and refreshing.

I wonder if the extra senselenses were intended to deter trespassers. After a year, I can't remember much else about these clients. I'm not even sure what they do, or how they could afford this huge complex.

Maybe the senselenses mask Rein's scent. It's a small hope, but I grab onto it. At least no branches of the path lead here. We should be safe.

Rein makes a spitting sound. I hear something wet hit the floor, pink light filling the darkness. "Don't ever make me eat clay again."

Their voice is clearer without the teeth covers. I find their false eyes. My legs are shaking. "Sorry. It was the only way."

They nod. "Well, it worked as much as it could. Now what?"

I look around. I can sense the cavernous ceiling above us, but Rein's light isn't sufficient to show more than the immediate walls and furnishings. Our voices echo, making me uneasy. I'm used to smaller spaces, every wall close enough to touch.

"This is as far as I thought," I admit when my breath has settled more or less into its normal rhythm.

"Great."

I push off the wall, taking Rein's hand. It feels less repulsive than before, bandaged and fitting neatly in mine. "Come on. Let's get further in. And then ..." I wonder if we left a trail through the trees. A transport will have artificialights. Rein's fingers tighten around mine.

"And then?"

My skin tingles. "I need to know exactly what's happening. I need to know what to expect ..."

"When they find me," they finish. I look at them. Their face is half clay, half pink light. I see the exhaustion on their lips. I smell the sickness on their breath.

"Maybe," I say, trying to believe my words. *How far did we run? Was it far enough?* "We have time."

They can't see me, but I feel them watching as I lead us through the darkness of a place I made.

I BRING us to a room on the second floor, in the middle of the complex. The only feature is a small window high up on the wall. I designed this room with multiple purposes in mind. Some possibilities I suggested to the clients were: cultivation, storage, or hobby projects. The purpose of the window is not to let light in (of course) but fresh air. It can be opened with the aid of a rod, which I find in a holder on the wall. *At least I can use that as a weapon.*

Besides the rod, the room is unfurnished. Rein finds the wall and sits down on the floor. I join them, watching their face. They draw a breath through chapped lips tinged red. I'm gripped by a sudden fear they'll die here, in front of me. It won't matter if the transport finds our trail. Everything they know will be lost, buried—again?

Twenty-four hours ago, I imagined I knew things. I was good at my job, and I read a lot. I especially liked learning history. Sitting next to Rein in a room lit by their teeth, I wonder if I ever knew anything worthwhile at all.

"Do the machines stretch across the sky?" I ask. It's not the first thing I wanted to say, but I've been trying to picture them: a layer of metal machines hovering on the other side of the clouds.

Rein shakes their head. "Each tower has solar-powered platforms, spinners attached by chains. These generate the clouds. Towers are arrayed across the Clouding area."

I nod, adopting their habit of visual cues even though they

can't see me. This at least tallies with history I've learned. "The towers cover the world."

Rein turns to me. Their mouth twitches. "No. Only part of the world has clouds. The rest is exposed."

I stare at them. "That's not true."

They laugh, rough and bitter. "I should know. I grew up there."

I don't have a response to this. They pick at the bandages on their fingers. "We had some thin cloud when I was a kid. As I grew, it got thinner and thinner, until there wasn't any. Just sun, burning bright."

In the semi-dark, I picture it: white hot, like an artificia-light turned to the highest possible brightness. I imagine heat prickling my skin, like Rein's remembered burns.

Their voice is soft, steeped in recollection. "We moved into caves, smearing cream on our skin to protect it as best we could. Our tower cast a shadow, spinners rusted in place. Broken solar panels, smoothed by sandstorms tempered only by monsoons that flooded our homes and infected the burns."

I found my voice at last. "Couldn't the tower be fixed?"

They laughed again, more rasp than humor. "We thought so. That's what I signed up to do." They turn their teeth on me. "I volunteered, Mallory. I asked to go up there, fix the spinners and bring the clouds back."

My throat feels like sand. "What happened?"

"The Coalition lied to me. To all of us. They didn't put us to work on our tower. They brought us to yours."

I don't know what I expected. I found them in *my* forest, between *my* dead trees. It should've been obvious, once I learned the truth, where they fell from. But the notion of Rein working at the top of the tower—burning above while I walked below—sears me with uneasy guilt.

"Why?" is all I can croak.

"Your tower still worked," Rein murmurs, every word changing the shape of the gloom. "Using me, the Coalition diverted the last of my tower's energy to yours. My hands disconnected the last wires protecting my home from the sun. And when I found out what I'd done, what they were really using me for, I…"

As if remembering something, they stop, turning away from me. I'm left in deeper darkness, groping for reason.

"That can't be right," I say. "How could the Coalition keep a secret this big?"

"It can't, not anymore." Rein's voice adopts a new harshness. I feel them outlining the distance between us, between the lives we've led. I realize now there's nothing I can say, no reason to argue. All I can do is watch them peel away the gauze I used to cover their scars.

"A year ago, I got moved from spinner repair to shuttling materials."

I stay silent this time. Rein's teeth shine as they talk. "There are these open shuttles. We load them with cloud canisters to fuel the spinners. They're shipped up the towers from plants on the surface. I'm not sure what's in them, but I know how it smells. And what it does to you, after long enough." Their teeth flash, bared in place of words.

"Shuttlers drive between the platforms," they continue. I don't think they need me here to listen. Their story is enough, filling the room and proving itself realer than the walls I sculpted into being.

"One of us pilots the shuttle while the other loads and unloads," Rein says. "We're not watched closely. Over the past couple of years, it seemed there were fewer overseers. I think the protective suits are running out. Maybe they can't get the materials to make them anymore. I don't know. But during the past few months, we saw a chance.

"When we delivered canisters, we spread information. Ambition. And a time."

Rein exhales, sliding into a bout of coughing. I start to touch them, but change my mind. I let them cough alone.

When they catch their breath, they turn to me, clay eyes vacant. I feel exposed in their empty stare. "The time was two days ago. We loaded the shuttles with all the workers we could fit, picking them up from each platform. We smashed the panels driving the spinners. We threw canisters into the blades, jamming them beyond repair. Before the overseers could stop us, the pilots dove."

A new truth is dawning. I know what Rein meant now. *Final hours.* Fear of saying it aloud grips me as they continue, the last of their story spilling out into the air.

"I'd never been in the clouds before. I couldn't breathe. People were gagging, falling off the shuttle. I don't know what happened to the other shuttles—we spread out as much as possible—but we lost a few before we made it under the clouds.

"We could breathe then. But the pilot said it was dark. They couldn't see where they were going. The shuttles have no lights on them, and ... we crashed."

Rein works the gauze from their middle finger, balling it up in their fist. "I was thrown. I'm not sure who heard the crash, but I'm sure the shuttle was the first thing to be erased. Anyone who was there is probably dead. I got as far away as I could."

Their voice falters into silence, light dimming as their mouth closes. I sit beside them, remembering that first glimpse of pink between the trees. Listening to a report of the transport crash on the other side of the forest as I worked on my clay models, only half paying attention.

Bile stings my throat as I wonder how many other stories I've accepted, trusting the United Governments to tell me the truth about the world. After all, it's thanks to the United

Governments that the Clouding happened. "A treaty to protect humanity," the Coalition was famous for saying.

But which part of humanity got protection?

"You broke the tower," I say, barely putting shape to the words. "My tower."

Rein doesn't face me. "It was the only way."

"How long?" I ask. I can see the world they grew up in—cloudless and cruel. I superimpose dead trees on desert, plant my apartment next to a cave. My imagination, so wonderful for designing beautiful buildings, betrays me by painting an all-too-realistic picture of what's to come.

"I don't know. Days, weeks—depends how much energy was stored in the fuel cells, how badly the spinners broke."

"But ..." I grope for hope. I can't picture it. "Why accept my help at all?"

Rein shifts. "It was the way you smelled."

Their answer confuses me, momentarily setting my terror aside. "Clay?"

They touch their manufactured face, leaving fingerprints. "In the caves, there was clay. We used to play with it, mold things. I don't think it really meant much to me at the time, but it was the coldest thing we had."

"I'm sorry."

Rein snorts, coughs. "If I were you, I wouldn't be sorry. You had a better life till now."

"But it was a lie." I can't stop looking at their hands, then mine. In pink light, they don't look so different. "The Clouding was supposed to protect *everyone*, and it was a lie. No one should be above the clouds, and no one should be outside of them. The Clouding failed." My imagination is sprinting now, drawing a new picture that's more real than anything I've sculpted. No matter how I turn it in my head, it doesn't go away.

I take Rein's hand, running my fingers over their

bandages. I'm not sure when it happened, but the heat of their skin doesn't bother me anymore. "Rein, I'm not sorry because I feel like I deserve what you did. Or that it was right. I'm sorry because I don't know if it's wrong, either."

Rein turns to me, teeth shining in my eyes. "When they find us, they'll try to cover it up. Get more workers up on the tower, repair the damage before you notice a difference. I—I was angry at everyone under the clouds. I wanted you to feel the sun like we did. Mallory, if we succeeded, it's almost worse than if we failed."

"Will they kill you?"

"They have to. I can't be trusted anymore."

"And who will take your place?"

Rein licks their lips. "I don't know. People might start disappearing from here."

"The clouds will thin. Rein, whether my tower fails or not, what you're saying is they're breaking. Here, where you grew up, across the whole world. It's only a matter of time before there aren't any towers left to repair. We'll all be exposed."

Rein pulls their hand from mine. "I won't live long enough to find out. You should get out of here, go back to your apartment and prepare. Leave me in this—house, is it?"

I'm cold. I sit back, looking around the little room. "A multi-family complex. I designed it for a client of BioHomes."

Rein scrambles to their feet. "BioHomes?!" Their voice is raw, full of cracks.

I get to my feet as well, alarmed. "Yes? That's the company I work for."

They reach for the wall, feeling for the door. I grab their elbow. "Rein, wait! What is it? What do you know about BioHomes?"

They pull away from me, frantic. "They're the ones who make them!"

"Make what?"

"The towers. The cannisters, the spinners. Shuttles—all of it."

The bottom drops out of my stomach. "Rein. You don't mean—"

"BioHomes *is* the Coalition."

White light bursts through the window, filling the room. I gasp, shading my shocked eyes from the beam. Outside, a voice calls through a speaker.

"YOU ARE ON BIOHOMES PROPERTY. THIS AREA IS SEALED. OFFICERS ARE ENTERING TO DETAIN ALL TRESPASSERS."

I CAN'T SEE. Light swims in my eyes and I fumble towards the door to the little room. "Rein?"

Someone grabs me. I almost scream, but the sound seizes in my throat. Charred lips brush my ear. "You have to hide."

"Rein." I find their arms wrapped in my bandages, my clothes. "I know this place. Please—stay with me."

I hold a map of the complex in my mind. I close my eyes against the artificialights. I can find my way better with my other senses. Oriented by the room we left, I turn towards the stairs, pulling Rein with me. They don't move.

"Mallory, there's nowhere to go. They'll sense me, but you might be able to hide. I'll tell them I was alone."

I hear doors open on the lower level. I lean close to Rein, taste the burning on their breath. "I'm not leaving you to them." In the back of my panicked brain, I think: *I don't want to face the sun alone.*

When it comes down to it, I'm healthier and stronger. I drag Rein after me. "I designed this place," I hiss, pushing them in front of me up the stairs. "I know every space."

Below us, I hear feet climbing other stairs. I push Rein to the landing and take the lead again, running along hallways I sculpted out of clay. There are no windows here, so I open my eyes. I let Rein's teeth guide us through the complex, to the far side on the edge of the dead forest. I open a door and bring us through two connected rooms. Where a tool case will be, I find an open panel. I push Rein inside and close the panel behind me, locking us into the space between walls.

For a moment, our breathing is all I hear. Then, distantly, I catch voices calling to one another. Footsteps reverberating through the floor. In the crack where the panel meets the wall: the wild beams of artificialights.

I try to keep my breathing measured, regular. Rein seems to be holding their breath. When the beams cross over the crack in front of us, I flinch away, causing Rein to shift further along the wall.

They're close, but not in this room. They haven't come so far. I hope they decide not to search this end of the complex. Maybe they'll just sweep through with the artificialights. They won't think we could hide so well—will they?

Rein grabs my wrist. I jerk, looking at them. Their voice is a croak.

"*Listen.*"

I hold my breath. Something crackles, like flame. After a few seconds, I realize it's static. A strange, automated snapping sound. It's moving slowly, but definitely getting closer.

"Detector," Rein gasps. My pulse hitches.

I remember the pulses on the path, the way the transport found us too fast. The Coalition can do more than manipulate bacteria. They brought a tool to detect radiation. Despite my hope, the senselenses couldn't mask Rein's radioactivity. A mere wall will do nothing.

I push Rein further along the inside of the wall, away from the panel. We end up against the outer wall. If BioHomes removes the panel and comes after us, we'll have nowhere to run.

The static pulses come closer. A room away, maybe two. With them I hear voices.

"What if they're dead? After crashing, not many survived."

"If they're dead, we'll take the body. No problem."

"They might not be alone." This is a third voice, carrying authority.

Footsteps enter the last room. I hold my breath. Rein has gone silent beside me.

"They were definitely here," the first voice says. Static draws close to the wall. "Maybe left through the window."

"We'll find them outside if so," says the second voice.

"Or they didn't leave," the third voice says. They're close to the wall now. "Bring a sledgehammer."

"Yes, Arden." Footsteps leave the room. The static remains. I close my eyes. This is it.

Three tones ping on the other side of the wall. "Yes?" Arden says, answering the call. The silence is brief. "*Fuck!*"

"Arden?"

"Fucking *fuck* fuck. I don't fucking believe it." The wall shakes as someone kicks it. I stiffen, grabbing Rein's arm. "Those fuckers took the overseer emergency shuttles as they were trying to evacuate. There's been another attack."

"What?! When?"

"Not ten minutes ago. Security up there is crippled, three more spinners down."

The floor lurches under us. Not far from the complex, something explodes, shaking the walls on either side of us. Rein falls into me and I struggle to hold them up in the narrow space between walls. In the room beyond, Arden's swears reach a new pitch.

"That was close. Get over to the crash site before government does. Keep that thing on!"

Footsteps recede, beams of artificialight fading from the gap by the panel. The crackling detector becomes quieter, and is gone.

We're left in pink-tinged gloom, Rein's head resting on my shoulder. I breathe in gasps, not sure whether I feel lucky or more doomed than before.

One thing is clear: we can't stay here.

"Come on." I half-drag Rein back to the panel. I chance a few seconds of tense listening before pushing it out and climbing back into the room. Muddy footprints mar the floor, showing where the BioHomes officers were standing just moments before.

"I fucking knew it."

I spin, heart in my throat. I find myself looking down the barrel of a gun. Rein stands beside me, false eyes staring.

The Coalition officer wears a uniform not unlike Rein's, but where their number had been, the officer's chest is bare. "Two for the price of one," they say with a sneer, looking me up and down. *Arden*, I think, putting a name to them. "You look strong. I'll give you a choice, then."

I try and fail to swallow. "Rein lives."

"Who?"

Light brightens as Rein smiles without humor. "Me."

Arden glares at them. "No point in naming a corpse." They point the gun at Rein, meeting my gaze. "You've got a chance to live, though. I can offer you a job."

My hands curl into fists, useless at my sides. "What job?"

Arden jerks their head up. "Your terrorist friend caused some damage to the tower. Could use a skilled worker to fix it."

Trembling, I shake my head. "No."

The gun swings back to me. "Then you die together."

Rein—uncannily still throughout the threats—lunges forward. Arden aims at them too late, the gun knocking Rein's shoulder and firing at the ceiling. At the same time, Rein's shining teeth bite down on their arm. Arden screeches, more rage than pain.

I've never fought anyone. The gunshot cracks in my ears, disorienting me. Rein surprised Arden, but they're injured and weak. They can't win this fight alone.

I lurch into action, chasing the waving gun. Another shot barely misses me, the nearness splitting my senses to bits. I grab Arden's wrist, push with all my strength. We fall back.

Fresh drywall collapses under the weight of three bodies. Arden vanishes under debris. I don't know if they're unconscious or dead. I peel the gun from their hand and pull Rein back. Together, we run.

There are still lights outside. My thoughts spin in dizzying circles. I throw the gun out a window, scared of the weight of it. We can't use the main door, I think, holding Rein's shaking shoulders. I take them down the stairs in the back, bringing us to the level below Arden. I remember putting an emergency exit here, since it's so far from the main door. I see it now for the first time in the pink light of Rein's panting.

Pouring everything I have into not stopping on this side of the door, I push the crash bar and hurl us out into the not-all-dark. The artificialights are focused on the other side of the complex. In front of us, the pale shapes of dead trees disappear into shadow, except for one anomaly. Some are on fire.

Rein wheezes. Smoke is thick on the air. "Shuttle crash."

"That's where BioHomes was heading," I gasp, adrenaline stuttering my speech. "We have to go the other way."

I pivot, facing a narrow stretch of darkness between artificialights and burning trees. In crossing it, we run the risk of encountering BioHomes officers on their way to the crash. I strain to see the far side of the crash site. Between the trees I glimpse the dim light of the walkway, vibrating on a rise beyond the complex.

Who knows who will come from that way, drawn by the noise and light? I have to hope they won't be Coalition, at least. I drag Rein towards the strip of trees between the walkway and the burning shuttle.

Our pace is slow. Rein is barely conscious, stumbling on my feet and tripping over mushrooms. I feel fresh blood on their hands. I don't know if it's theirs or Arden's. I don't know where we're going. *Just away.*

I try to watch and listen and feel all at once. One sense dominates the others: I smell smoke, and something else.

On my left, dead trees burn. I look over, flames dazzling the darkness. Rein trips, tumbling away from me. I try to catch them and I trip too, falling into the cold embrace of the mushrooms.

Something hot rests against my ankle. "Rein?" I follow the soft glow of their teeth to where they lie, breathing slowly with their face in the dirt. One of the eyes I molded for them is squashed out of shape. I pull them up, searching the darkness for what tripped us.

A body, silhouetted against distant fire. Rein groans. They can smell what I smell: charred flesh.

"Who is it?"

I lean them against a tree and crawl over to the body. They smell of smoke and sickness. Familiar blisters cover their skin.

"Number," Rein gasps behind me. I swallow, turning a face scorched beyond recognition. Only the final three digits are readable, the rest of their uniform burned away.

"796."

"Tether," Rein says, voice breaking.

I sit back, staring at what was once a person. "They're dead. I'm sorry." A broken bone juts from their leg, colored with fire and blood. I try to keep myself from gagging. No way they crawled this far with that injury. "I think they were thrown, before the crash."

Rein is sobbing. My head and body ache. Every sound hurts my ears. Smoke sears my lungs and throat and light echoes dance in my eyes.

The boost adrenaline gave is dissolving into exhaustion. I want to sink into the ground, be covered with mushrooms before the sun burns them away. Nothing will get fixed, I realize. If the Coalition—if BioHomes—clears away all of it, smooths it over like nothing happened, what about next year? What about tomorrow?

What then?

I drag myself from Tether's corpse. Rein covers their face, wiping away clay eyes incapable of producing tears. I wrap my arms around them, trying to pull them up. They push me back.

"No! Leave me."

My voice hitches. "We c-can't stay. They're going to sweep the area, find all the bodies ..."

"Let me be one of them."

I don't know if it's smoke or fear or grief that burns my insides. I don't know if it's me or Rein, clay melting like skin.

Their fingers dig into my forearms. "Mallory, this is it. You can't save me. You can't fix this. It'll end in fire."

The ache in my throat climbs into my mouth, forces the words out. "Then I'll burn with you."

Artificialights cut across the darkness. Rein can't see or feel them, but they can hear the footsteps running down the slope from the path. I hold onto them even as they try to push me off.

"Go, Mallory!"

"STAY WHERE YOU ARE."

Lights blind me and force the waiting tears from my eyes. Rein's grip goes slack. Everything turns white.

THE FIRST MORNING I witness is dark gray. Light trickles through thinning clouds, revealing the landscape outside the detention center. I don't know how to describe it—widespread light, with no clear source. It's like the underworld.

And why not? I thought at first I was dead.

The past week has been a blur of interrogation. Gloved hands taking tests, crackling machines measuring my level of exposure. Suited bodies asking questions that have no answers. Questions that should never have needed to be asked. And when I tried to ask my own back, I was told to be silent. It was bigger than me, they said. It was bigger than Rein.

I see them now, on the other side of my eyes. Lying against the tree, raw in the light of white beams. Mouth open, chest still.

In my mind, I try again and again to rouse them. I stare at their chest, waiting for it to move. I put my hand against their mouth and feel for breath.

My efforts are wasted. I'm never able to reach them. I'm never able to find out if they're alive. And in an endless string of interviews, no one will tell me where they are. My questions are shoved aside in favor of others—which go nowhere.

"How long have you worked for BioHomes?"

"Why didn't you take the victim to the hospital?"

"Why did you run?"

"You didn't own the property. Using default codes before the owner has a chance to change them is equivalent to breaking in."

"This should have been reported to the United Governments immediately."

"What makes you think you were equipped to act the way you did?"

Every question is more accusation than inquiry. I'm tired of talking about BioHomes, outlining again and again what I knew, what I didn't. Don't they see? Nothing like that can happen without government protection. Yet each time I try to press deeper, a wall is erected.

"The United Governments is investigating the issue. You need not concern yourself with specifics."

"Leave this to the proper authorities. Thank you for your statement."

"Rest assured that your concerns have been heard and passed along."

I don't believe for a moment BioHomes' actions were secret. But the agents don't care what I believe.

According to the federal investigators, BioHomes sold an image of sustainable Clouding. According to the United Governments, the workers received proper care and compensation. All were supposed to be outfitted with protective suits, like the overseers. According to official records, the unclouded regions have been unoccupied for decades.

And why weren't we told the clouds were shrinking? It wasn't relevant, they said. No one was supposed to live on those continents.

They're all lying. I know it. They've been lying for eighty years, and now the clouds are thinning.

After a week, I'm released—sort of. An agent trails me through the detention center. I'm not done talking, not until my testimony is used to indict the Coalition and wipe the United Governments clean of corruption. I've been given a new name: Hawley. They gave me a choice of last names. From the white list they handed me, I chose Rain.

It's close. Close as I can get.

"You can't go home," my agent tells me as we walk through the detention center, gray light forcing its way through the open shutters. "Until the trials are over, your life could be in danger. Your new address is protected, along with your new name."

I know too much. *I know nothing.* I think about my empty apartment, too small. Will my new place be larger? Will it have windows to let in the encroaching light?

I know what it won't have: a glass smeared with antiseptic gel. Bloodstained clothes in the bin. A bowl sitting abandoned on my bed.

All the evidence of Rein will be gone—burned away.

My agent brings me to the desk before the detention center doors. It's strange, seeing the person in front of me in pale, sourceless light. They look weak. We all do.

"Hawley Rain," they say, spinning a pad around for me to sign. I press my fingers to it and they take it back, handing me a cuff. "This should disrupt most tracking. Whitnall will escort you to a transport to your new residence."

My agent steps up next to me. I can't help but feel like their presence is just as much about keeping me under control as protecting the secrets I hold. "When you're ready."

After everything, I'm surprised to realize I don't want to leave, not until I know what happened to Rein. They were so sick ... I still feel their blisters against my palm, see the twisted skin of their face.

This pale light is just the beginning. Outside the detention center, I'll be exposed to the first beams of solar radiation to penetrate the clouds. Soon, every face will match Rein's.

I want to ask about this agent about them, beg again to see them. Are they here, or in a hospital? Are they dead?

I fear to ask that question. And I know my agent won't tell me either way. The United Governments refuse to permit me this final truth. It's as if Rein never existed.

Whitnall waits behind me. I gather my new identity and walk past the desk. We leave the detention center, stepping out into nether light. I'm loaded into an armored transport, Whitnall taking the seat beside me. I watch the detention center until it's out of sight.

Overhead, the clouds thin.

MY NEW HOME is nearly twice the size of my apartment. It feels like a bribe. The senselens is pre-programed to smell like clay. The first thing I do is change the settings.

Nothing smells like Rein. The closest I come is a mix of smoke and antiseptic. Even this is false, an approximation. The antiseptic was me, the smoke the crash. No matter how I try, I can't mimic their real scent. There's no option for radiation.

The new home has a stock of clay and my old things collected in a box in the middle of the main room. Some clothes are missing—the clothes Rein was wearing when I saw them last.

I unpack because I don't know what else to do. I arrange my small collection of things and repeat my new name to myself.

"Hawley Rain, Hawley Rain. Rain. Rain."

When there's nothing left in the box, I unwrap the clay. It gives to my touch.

I tear a piece away and look around. A file on the table tells me about my new job. I'm one of a team of designers: some from BioHomes and smaller companies, others freelancers.

Our task is to fix this. Find a solution before the clouds disperse entirely, and our region burns.

Clay in one hand, I flip through the file and contemplate our options. We can redesign the towers, remake the broken spinners. Maybe. If we can mimic the parts, if the designs still exist to follow. But even then, who will work them? Who will fix them when they break?

We can't repeat the Coalition's mistake.

I look at the other proposed solutions, typed out in cold print on flat sheets I'm not used to. So quickly, we revert to navigating by light. I run my fingers over the words, but feel nothing. The loss hurts, somehow. Like the world is smaller, cheaper than it was in darkness.

We can build a dome over our heads. We can move in on other regions, overcrowd ourselves until those towers wear out too. There are fewer safe spaces every day. Rebellion rippled from region to region, and where it didn't touch, workers were removed after the Coalition's exposure. It's only a matter of time.

Reading the possibilities, I peel a chunk of clay away from the block. I start molding it with no idea how to begin to undo the damage of ages.

At the end of the day, light fading at last, I hold a small face, melted skin where eyes should be.

DURING THE FIRST MONTH, we call it twilight. In the second, it becomes dusk. In the third, it is afternoon. My eyes adjust to the brightness, but my skin burns. Even at night, I feel it. Radiation reaching through the little veil we pulled across our world.

I have nightmares. I'm burning, Rein's drowning. Blisters cover my skin and Rein sinks into darkness, the light of their mouth swallowed by black waves. I wake up sweating. I can't get the scent of water out of my nose. I'm stuck at the complex, that last moment of intimacy we had. The last time we were alone.

Had it really only been a few hours? I've never known anyone as deeply. I've never remembered a face so well.

I push back the covers and walk. Some distant lights mar the darkness, and even night isn't as pure as the world under the Clouding. Outside, moonlight slips between thinner and thinner clouds.

I breathe the air outside, searching for bioluminescence. It began fading as soon as the light returned. Bacteria stopped casting their blues into the gloom. Mushrooms seemed paler. Now, standing outside my little lie of a house, I see only false light. Lights in distant houses like mine. Moonlight reflected on the clouds, which is really just sunlight reflected twice.

Even at night, the sun watches us.

I stand outside for as long as I can, grateful the stab of solar radiation is gone from my skin. Still, I feel its heat lingering in the dark. Waiting for dawn.

I close my eyes and try to think of a solution. Plants that lay dormant for decades have crept back out of the soil, only to turn brown as the sunlight worsens. The world, freshly reborn, balances on the cusp of death.

I can no longer stand the light of the moon. I retreat inside, locking the door behind me. Whitnall cautions me to keep a low profile. While the United Governments believe all main players in BioHomes' corruption are in custody, there's no way of accounting for the depth of conspiracy. I won't be truly safe until after the trials. And maybe never.

Does it matter, with the sun growing stronger each day?

My bed isn't appealing. I'll only have more nightmares. Instead I turn to work.

I sit at my desk and begin molding clay. I could use digital tools, LED projections, and algorithms to speed up the process—but clay connects me to my previous life. Clay lets me feel.

I start by building a tower. The towers still stand; they're about all that remains of the Clouding. Undamaged panels still pump solar power into the grid, fueling the generators of greenhouses and air purification systems. As the clouds dissipate, these processes will become less crucial. If we can't adapt, they'll become obsolete.

My tower grows. I roll wires and affix them to the base. I

imagine what the top looks like. Clouds still obscure it, but we can see a shadow.

A dome is ridiculous, but maybe a screen—stretched from tower to tower. The amount of material needed would be extensive. And the type—something that could withstand sunlight, endure for years—it would have to be like the overseers' suits, which seem to have become less effective over time. Whatever amalgamation of materials they used wasn't perfect, and to try and produce it on a gigantic scale ...

I place my palm on the top of my little tower of clay. I press down, collapsing it into a shapeless mound.

In the lump, I see a face.

When I can't sleep, I sculpt them. First I made a small model, then a bust. I look over at it, standing shadowy in the window. It's complete, and not. It's missing my additions.

Peeling the pieces of my tower apart, I recreate the false eyes, remembering how they looked in pink light. I can feel the skin underneath, hot with sickness. I close my eyes, cradling Rein's in my palms.

My thumbs trace their edges, soft and cool. They're not so different from the senselenses I used to make for houses. I've sculpted so many of those. But not anymore. They're not in demand now that everyone has turned to sight instead.

I regret that change, maybe more than the others. Senselenses were always my favorite parts to design. Mixing scents until I reached the perfect balance, then sending a vial of oil to Jayde to forward to the client for approval. They were always impressed. Even if I didn't like the project, or the scents themselves, I took pride in that step.

Unlike the complex, I think suddenly. Eight senselenses, so overpowering in their output, the potent aroma of water. I'd never dreamed they could create that experience. That oppression.

I'm dragged back there: air thicker than it should be, the two of us wading through a cloud of—a cloud—*cloud* ...

My hands close around the false eyes, crushing them into new shapes.

IN THE FOURTH month after the spinners ceased running, the clouds just a wisp overhead, I gather with my fellow designers in a building that once belonged to BioHomes.

"The towers that held the fans still stand." I set my clay model on the table, my fingerprints scattered up and down its struts. "What we need is something small, automated, that can run continuously, without the issues the platforms had. Those machines were built nearly a century ago. We should never have been trying to keep them going. BioHomes was so focused on old technology, they forgot what we've developed since."

I open the small plastic case I've brought. The clay forms inside remind me of eyes.

"With a small addition of modern technology, we might be able to create the same effect. Even a better effect." I press the circular forms onto the clay towers.

Jayde frowns. *Not Jayde anymore,* I remind myself. Their new name is Thyme. It's an adjustment for both of us, working together as equals. "Senselenses?"

"On a larger scale," I say, looking from them to the other designers. We all know how senselenses work to spread aromas around buildings, creating a recognizable sensual footprint. We've lived with them, designed them, sold them. But have we ever truly looked at them? "We previously employed senselenses widely, diffusing scented vapor on a small scale. If we make them larger, and change the vapor to a gas concoction that blocks radiation, we can use them to make a layer that protects us, but doesn't block light itself."

The designers shift and I feel their energy: months of tension unspooling into hope.

"We'd need production plants on the ground," Thyme says, tapping rapidly on a pad. They stop, meeting my eyes. Their face is peeling, light burns marring their hands. We all have them, now.

"But ... it might work." Thyme smiles, tentative. I feel my lips mimic theirs. It's been so long since I felt hope.

"It's a chance," I say.

A chance is all we ever had.

THE TRIAL BEGINS TODAY. A transport comes to collect me, covering me in body armor and driving me to the detention center. Agents flank me, Whitnall among them. They sit with me in an individual witness waiting room. The first day will cover testimony by BioHomes employees. I'll testify third.

My time comes. I'm led through sparse hallways, sunlight slanting through the windows. It burns.

Construction of my modified senselenses has begun on the towers, but it won't be finished until the end of the year. Only a thin layer of cloud protects us now. We can all see the sun on the other side.

I've started developing blisters if I'm outside too long. I bind them with gel and gauze, the smell capturing my memory. I wash my hands over and over again.

In the courtroom, a box holds nearly twenty Coalition members. I recognize Arden, though this is the first time I'm seeing their face clearly. If they had bruises from our fight, they've long since faded, leaving burns in their place.

I meet their eyes through my mask, wondering how things

might've gone differently. If Arden had killed Rein, and killed me too, it wouldn't have stopped the United Governments from exposing what was happening. It would have meant nothing.

I look from one face to another, most unfamiliar. These are the major players, those who ordered everything that happened with the towers. They have never been above the clouds. Their skin was clear.

No one's skin is clear now.

Twenty faces, blistered by sun. So few, when it comes down to it. There will be separate trials for those who carried out what these twenty asked. Those who acted as overseers, clad in anonymous white suits. The suits are gone now, those faces likewise exposed.

I'm called to take my place in the witness box. My heart thuds in my chest as Whitnall trails me to my place. I stand, facing the accused, the jury, the government officers, the judges in their blue robes. I hear the whine of a recorder and see lenses facing me. My face is covered by my body armor, my identity concealed as much as possible.

I draw a breath.

"You worked for BioHomes as a designer, is that correct?"

I face my questioner, recalling those first days in the detention center following the crash. I swallow against a dry throat.

"Yes. I designed private homes for clients."

"And how did you find out about the corrupt nature of BioHomes?"

I look around the courtroom. So many faces. None of them is the one I search for. "I met someone who'd escaped the clouds. Their name was Rein."

Hour by hour, I tell the court what happened. I remember it so clearly, though it was nearly a year ago now. I start with Rein, with pink teeth in the dark.

It all starts with Rein.

I speak about them in the past tense, make them part of the story. It hurts less that way.

The last I saw, Rein was lying against a dead tree, arms limp in their lap.

It's an image that fills my nightmares.

For two hours, I stand witness. I'm examined. Cross-examined. Dismissed. Escorted back to the little room. After three more hours, they send me home.

I don't need to attend the rest of the trial. In fact, I'm advised against it. It'll last weeks, my agent tells me. I should focus on my work instead.

They bring me home, unstrap my body armor and drive away. Sun burning my face, I retreat inside.

At my desk, I check on the tower progress to distract myself from the wounds the trial opened. We're in the final stages of troubleshooting while construction finishes. I run simulations, curtains drawn across my windows. They do little to keep the heat out. I sweat at my pad.

I do all my work digitally now. My clay I use only for art.

I'M SCULPTING THEM, from the face down.

I add to my bust, buying a wire frame to hold their arms. I sculpt their legs around rods and position them, wetting the clay and smoothing the connections between pieces. In sunlight I close my eyes, remember the feel of their body under my hands as I covered their skin with gel and bandages.

I order more clay. I keep running out.

Studies fill my house. Their hands, their lips. Their face, again and again. I never get the lines right, the divots where their eyes once were. When I'm frustrated, I recreate their false face. At least that I know by heart. But it isn't them. None of the sculptures are them.

Still, I make more.

I wrap some of the sculptures in gauze. I apply bandages where I remember wounds. I sculpt blisters and then smooth them out, imagining healing skin that never had a chance to mend itself. I put some sculptures in the closet, let them stand in darkness. I make hands and put them in water. I make sure to always keep the water cold.

From a box I never fully unpacked, I find my best clothes. I dress the one full-size sculpture, its arms wrapped in unstained gauze. I don't put false eyes on this one. I leave it twisted. I leave it true.

The night I dress the sculpture, I cry myself to sleep.

AFTER THE BIOHOMES employees have testified, surviving cloud workers describe the conditions at the towers. I try to go, but security won't let me in. No audience is allowed at the trial, even former witnesses. The information is too sensitive.

I don't know how many workers testified. I don't know their names. I don't know if Rein was among them.

At the end of the year, seventy-four BioHomes collaborators are indicted. All I can think about is Rein's number: 774. It's right, somehow. And terribly wrong.

I finish another bust. I place it on the table next to my bed. I've run out of clay again. My hands ache too much for me to work, so I sleep.

My curtains are no longer able to keep the sun from burning my face.

JUST ONE WEEK after the indictment, the modified senselenses are activated. They blow the last wisps of cloud away. The sun shines brightly, scorching the ground and roofs of homes. Wildfires ignite across the region. I stand inside and try to hold onto hope, while the news rages against this new invention, which has done nothing but blow away the last of our protection from the sun.

Grass browns and dies. Skin turns red—but it doesn't blister.

After a week, it doesn't even burn.

Fires are quenched and the news changes overnight. A success, it proclaims. We have tamed the sun.

Grass regrows brilliant green. Saplings unfurl tender leaves. Agricultural firms rediscover the old ways, spreading seeds that have a chance of surviving the season.

The design team is awarded titles, medals. I leave mine in its box, shoved under my bed next to the wall. The United Governments call the new year The Clearing. They celebrate a new era.

I want to believe them. Standing in a room filled with fragments of a ghost, I try so hard to believe in the future.

We're never told where the seventy-four indicted collaborators are sent. All trial witnesses are cautioned to maintain low profiles indefinitely, imprisoned in our false identities. In my standard house, I remain Hawley Rain.

The Clearing.

Filing the finished plans for the towers, I think about the name. Clearing of consciences, clearing of records. A back turned on the past, a promise not to repeat it. Millions of eyes fixed forward. We look up, blinded by the present and the future. Only when we blink can we see a brief image of the past—a flicker of darkness hiding on the other side of sight.

When I've packed everything about the trial away, I stand outside my house and stare at the sun. It's not beautiful. It doesn't hurt like it once did, but it's not beautiful. I think about the bioluminescent shimmer of bacteria and mushrooms. I think about cool dark and soft enveloping silence.

Night isn't the same as what we had before. It's brief, stuffy. The bacteria don't luminesce anymore. The paths have been switched off.

The Clearing. It's a small truth, double-edged.

Insects whine and leaves rustle. A transport stops on the road behind me, door opening and closing. Distantly, a different engine roars.

City noises are another thing I struggle to get used to. I may never be allowed to take back my real name or move. Many lower-tier Coalition members escaped indictment. They're out in the world now, freer than I am. Breathing clean air.

The Clearing.

Who's in the clear, really?

When my eyes sting and spots fill my vision, I look away from the sun. I have to accept that I did something good, but it doesn't feel any better than what I did before. I don't feel like anything's been fixed.

Sweating in the heat, I turn to go inside. Behind me, footsteps crunch on gravel.

"Mallory?"

I stumble, turning too fast at the shape of my name. My mind swims, my vision still patchy. Someone is walking towards me. I back up, afraid to believe—

"It's you." Rein's voice is clearer than I've ever heard it.

I blink the light echoes away. They're standing in front of me: whole, scarred, sightless. Their teeth shimmer. I think— but no, they no longer hold a light of their own. It's just the sun, reflecting.

"How—I thought—" I can't get the words out. My throat

folds in on itself, clay collapsing into shapelessness. "How did you find me?"

Rein sways and I worry—but it's emotion, not sickness, that grips them. "They wouldn't tell me where you were," they say, voice trembling. "I wasn't allowed anywhere until the trial finished, and then ... I've been to every designer I could find. But you're not listed as that. You're under—"

"Sculptor," I finish, breathless. I'm afraid to move, afraid this image will melt away.

Their face, their hands, their body. I've made them so many times, turned pieces of them over in my hands. Looking at them now—I realize I've forgotten how their features look in skin, not clay.

Rein smiles. Their scars remain, but the blisters are gone. The blood is gone. They're alive. Rein—here, in front of me —*alive*.

"I found your surname: Rain. And I thought, well, maybe ..." They draw a shaky breath, closing the distance between us, arms out, feeling for what they can't see. "And then I smelled you. And I knew."

My hands are shaking. I reach up, touching their face. Their skin is soft, warmer than the clay I molded from memory.

"I thought you died," I gasp.

Rein's hands find my cheeks, smearing my tears. "You were ready to burn with me."

I grab onto them, processing the realness of their body, the way it fits so perfectly against mine. I bury my face in their chest, inhaling their scent.

It's changed. No longer sick, they smell like sunlight.

"We won't burn," I say, my throat aching and wonderful. "No one will."

ACKNOWLEDGMENTS

This novella owes its existence to the natural world it attempts to capture. Whether you read these words in a nest of papers or on a screen, this book took numerous bodies to make. No stories written today can afford to ignore this aspect of their creation.

I am grateful for the trees that I grew up under, yet fearful for their future. We know that acknowledgement is not enough. And while we know too what must be done to stop the fire, we are afraid.

This is a story of regret as much as resilience, of reverence coupled with resentment. As you finish reading and return to the blindingly bright world, please remember: fiction has never been the opposite of truth.

The time to say thank you has passed. Now, we work.

ABOUT THE AUTHOR

Marisca Pichette writes across all biomes of speculation. Her 2023 poetry collection, *Rivers in Your Skin, Sirens in Your Hair*, was a finalist for the Bram Stoker and Elgin Awards. You can find Marisca's short stories and poetry in *Clarkesworld*, *Strange Horizons*, *The Magazine of Fantasy & Science Fiction*, *Asimov's*, *Nightmare Magazine*, and many other magical places. This is their first standalone work of long fiction. Marisca lives in Massachusetts, watching the stars.